OUR LITTLE SPARTAN COUSIN
OF LONG AGO

Chartas

The Little Cousins of Long Ago Series

OUR LITTLE SPARTAN COUSIN OF LONG AGO

Being the Story of Chartas, A Boy of Sparta

BY
JULIA DARROW COWLES

ILLUSTRATED BY
JOHN GOSS

NEW WEST PRESS

New West Press
Henderson, NV 89052
www.nwwst com

Ordering Information:
Special discounts are available on quantity purchases by corporations, associations, educators, and others. For details, contact the publisher at the listed address below.

U.S. trade bookstores and wholesalers: Please contact New West Press:

Tel: (480) 648-1061; or email: contact@nwwst.com

THIS STORY OF SPARTAN COURAGE

AND ENDURANCE

IS LOVINGLY DEDICATED TO

MY BROTHER

FRANK LOOMIS DARROW

Preface

———◆◇◆———

It has not been the intention of the author to confine the scenes of this story to a given date, but rather to select events which are typical of the Spartan life and character, and so to present a composite picture which is truly representative of a people unique in the history of mankind.

The story closes during the stirring times of the Persian invasion, but even here the author claims some of the license of the story-teller, though with no contradiction of fact, nor use of the imagination not fully warranted by Spartan history.

One of the objects sought has been to show the true nobility and rugged simplicity of the Spartan character, for it is scarcely credible that the citizens of the State which for so long a time was the acknowledged leader of all Hellas, could have been so wholly rude and savage as they are sometimes depicted.

Acknowledgment is hereby made of the author's indebtedness to "Miller's Dorians" for the invaluable aid which Professor Müller's comprehensive treatment has afforded.

Contents

———◆◇◆———

Pronunciation of Proper Names

A´gis

A-leu´as

An´dro-cles

A-pol´lo

As-sem´bly

A-the´na

A-the´ni-an

Ath´ens

Bras´i-das

Car-ne´a

Cas´tor

Ce´os

Char´tas

Cin´a-don

Cle-om´e-nes

Dan´a-us

Da-ri´us

Del´phi

Di´o-do´rus

Do´ri-ans

Do´rus

E-le´an

E´Hs

E-pho´re-um

Eu-ro´tas

Ge´lon

Gor´go

Greece

Hel´en

He´lots

Her´a-kles

Ho´mer

Hy´a-cin´thus

Il´i-ad

Ja´son

La-er´tes

Ly-cur´gus

Mar´a-thon

Me-lis´sa

Melon

Men-e-la´us

My´les

Od´ys-sey

O-lym´pi-a

O-lym´pi-ad

O-res´tes

Pan

Par´is

Pen´thi-lus

Per´sia

Persians

Pol´lux

Pro´cles

Pyr´rhic

Pyth´i-an

So´us

Spar´ta

Spar´tan

Sper´thi-as

Syl-la´ri-an

Tev-pan´der

The-og´nis

The´ron

The´seus (sus)

Troy

Zeus (zus)

CHAPTER I

A SPARTAN COMPANY

"A race! a race! Who will plunge first into Eurotas?"

The boy who shouted the challenge stood poised, ready for flight. His head was thrown back, his arms were extended, and one foot, thrust before him, touched the ground lightly.

It was Chartas who called, and at the sound of his voice the whole group of boys, fifteen in number, threw themselves into the same attitude, and, at a word, sped away to the banks of the river, Reaching there, they hastily threw off the one garment which each wore, and plunged into the stream.

"Chartas won!" they cried, as the challenger, whose lithe limbs gave him an advantage in running, splashed first into the water.

"He always wins in running," said Brasidas, "but wait till we wrestle. His speed will not count for so much then."

The splashing water almost drowned Brasidas' words, for the fifteen boys were swimming, ducking, plunging, and frolicking like a school of young porpoises.

However, Chartas had heard. "Yes," he answered, "I like to show my back in a race. 'Twould be different if 'twere a battle."

"How about your back now?" asked a mischievous boy named Gelon. As he spoke he dived quickly, caught Chartas by the ankles, and tripped him, face forward, into the water.

Chartas quickly recovered himself, dashed after Gelon, and a lively tussle followed. The water flew in all directions, and the other boys, quickly taking sides, began throwing water upon the two wrestlers, dashing it into the face of the one they hoped to see defeated.

The boys were well matched, but the river bottom was slippery, and as Gelon gave a turn to his antagonist's arms his foot slipped and he went down.

"Chartas wins! Chartas wins!" again shouted the boys, as Gelon came up sputtering, and shaking the water from his hair and eyes.

Gelon was not conquered, however, and he dashed once more upon Chartas. But at that moment, above the splashing of the water, and the shouting of the boys, a voice rang out from the river bank. "Back to the gymnasium; 'tis time for your drill!"

The voice was that of their iren, or captain,—a boy himself but little past twenty years,—whose name was Orestes.

Instantly the wrestling stopped, and the boys turned. Not a hand went back for a final splash, for these were Spartan boys, and the first lesson they had learned was *to obey*.

In a moment they had slipped into their chitons, and were hurrying toward the gymnasium.

As they started, Orestes threw his arm across the shoulders of Chartas, and the two followed a little more slowly.

"To-morrow the Assembly meets," said Orestes, "and I shall send you boys foraging. See how well you can acquit yourself, for I want to be proud of you."

"I wish I were old enough to attend the Assembly," said Chartas, "but I know you will tell me what takes place. I should like to listen to the speeches,—but then," he added, "it is rare sport to forage, and I shall do my best."

"I know you will," said Orestes, looking with genuine pride and affection at the younger boy.

When they reached the gymnasium the others were already selecting their quoits for throwing. They paid no heed to the open preference of their captain for Chartas, since every captain of boys in Sparta had his favorite pupil. The captain's favorite was given special training and special teaching; but he was not saved from hardships or dangers. If he had been, he would, himself, have hated it, and his companions would have held him in contempt. Instead, he was given harder tasks, and was thrown into greater dangers in order that he might gain courage and endurance, and be able to prove himself keen and unafraid. For these were the qualities which made the Spartans the most heroic men of all Greece.

"Now to your places," said Orestes, and, in a moment, the boys were ready for their exercises. There was no donning of gymnasium suits. The chiton was their one garment, worn on all occasions. It was a sleeveless shirt of wool.

Then began the exercise of quoit-throwing, in which each boy sought to send his quoit or discus with the best aim and to the greatest distance.

As one of the boys, named Theognis, took up his quoit, one of the smaller boys darted out of his place.

"Stand back!" shouted Theognis. "Do you want to play the part of Hyacinthus and be struck down?"

The boy retreated, and Theognis threw his quoit.

"Bravo!" cried the boys, for the discus had sped far beyond that of any other thrower.

Theognis threw back his head, as he stood erect. He was shorter than most of his company. He could never win in a race, and in wrestling he was often thrown; but his discus-throwing was always good, and he was glad to have won this "bravo "from the boys.

As the quoits were put away, Orestes turned suddenly to Theognis and said: "You referred a moment ago to Apollo and Hyancinthus. Tell us the story."

Theognis did not hesitate: "Hyacinthus was loved by the god Apollo, and they were often together. One day as they were playing at a game of quoits, Apollo threw his discus. It slipped from his hand, and, striking Hyacinthus, slew him. Apollo was deeply grieved. He had loved the beautiful boy, and now he was dead, slain by his own hand. But Apollo, god though he was, could not bring him back to life. So, where the blood of Hyacinthus had moistened the earth, he caused a beautiful purple flower to grow, and he named the flower the hyacinth."

"Your tale is as well told as your discus was well thrown," said Orestes, and once more Theognis felt a thrill of pleasure, for praise from one's captain was not easily gained in Sparta.

But though praise was not easily gained, it was a part of each boy's training to answer sudden and unexpected questions and to give his answers as clearly and as briefly as he could. This questioning taught him to think quickly and to express his thoughts readily. And so, though the Spartan boys were expected to be silent when with the older men, unless they were addressed, they learned to listen well, and to keep their minds alert, for a question might be put to them at the most unexpected moment, and it was a disgrace not to be able to answer quickly, briefly, and well.

CHAPTER II

THE ASSEMBLY

The streets of Sparta presented a lively scene on the following day

It was the monthly meeting of the Assembly, and every street was filled with a moving throng. Men of all ages were there, for every citizen who was old enough to bear arms could vote. The meeting was held in an open space just west of the city.

Sparta was ruled over by two kings and twenty-eight magistrates, who were called ephors. These thirty men could make plans, and propose changes in the government, but they must tell their plans to the whole people at one of the Assemblies, and let them vote "yes," or "no." In this way Sparta was governed.

Orestes and Procles, another captain of a company of boys, were together.

"The crowd is making way," said Orestes. "Yes," replied Procles, "the kings and ephors are taking their places."

The great gathering of people was made up principally of the men of Sparta, each dressed in his chiton, over which was draped the himation, or cloak. This cloak consisted of a square piece of cloth, sometimes" rounded at the corners. It was thrown over the left arm, brought loosely across the back under the right arm, and the end again thrown back over the left shoulder. Thus the right arm was left free, while the left was covered by the graceful drapery of the himation. Some of the men wore hats with a broad brim, but the greater number had their heads bare. All wore their hair long, and arranged in a knot upon the crown of the head.

Occasionally a young man would be seen with a purple military cloak, adding a brilliant bit of color to the scene. These cloaks were fastened with a clasp upon the right shoulder, where the ends fell apart, again leaving the right arm free and uncovered.

With the exception of these military cloaks, the people were dressed in white, for in Sparta it was said, "deceitful are dyes." The Spartans thought that nothing was so beautiful as the white color of the natural wool, and that dyes robbed the wool of its true beauty.

Occasionally, upon the outskirts of the crowd, or darting through the streets, would be seen a slave from the country, dressed in a leather cap, and a chiton made from skins. The workmen of the city, who had no vote in the government of Sparta, could readily be told by their simpler dress and their closely cut hair.

Orestes and Procles stood quietly among the men, their

arms folded beneath their cloaks, and their eyes cast down. Yet with quick glances they took note of any unusual sights.

"Who is the man in splendid garments, who has his hair parted and fastened with a jeweled ornament?" asked Procles quietly.

"He must be an ambassador—from Athens, perhaps," said Orestes.

"But see the gold and embroidery upon his cloak. I think he must come from beyond Greece," Procles replied.

"Perhaps he will speak, and then we will learn more about him," said Orestes.

Then one of the ephors arose, and the people became quiet. He made a short speech, and ended by proposing the name of a well-known citizen for councillor. Then he asked for the vote of the Assembly. The citizen was well liked, and when the vote was called for, the voices of the people arose in one great shout: "Aye, aye."

Then the man of whom Orestes and Procles had spoken was allowed to address the people. He was an ambassador, as they had guessed, and came from an island to the east of Greece. He wanted to arrange a treaty between his country and Sparta, but his appearance did not please the Spartans.

"He smells of ointments, and his clothes are far too richly embroidered," growled an old man, who stood near the boys.

"And he would have us Spartans pay for the extravagance which we allow not in our own country," replied the man to whom he had spoken.

There were murmurs of disapproval from the crowd while the ambassador spoke, and when the ephor called for a vote giving consent to the treaty, a few voices answered, but when it was asked whether they should deny the request, a multitude of voices blended like the roar of a mighty sea.

When it had grown quiet again, another of the ephors spoke. He told of a war in which one of their colonies was engaged. "They are losing ground," he said, "and they beg us to send them the statues of the Twin Gods, that they may bring them better fortune, and turn the tide of battle in their favor."

At this some of the people shouted, "Send them! Send them!" Others said, "No, no; it is too great a risk." "The statues might be lost at sea!" exclaimed others. "Let them make statues of their own!" "Why should we send them ours?"

The whole multitude was in an uproar. The angry voices increased; the excitement grew each moment. In vain the ephors tried to quiet the people. Even the kings could not control them. They threw up their arms; they shouted; they surged back and forth.

Suddenly a man vaulted to a place beside the ephors. In his hand he held a cithara, and he began to play. Then, to the accompaniment of his instrument, he sang.

No sound reached the multitude. Only those who looked knew that he was singing. But, one by one, these pointed, or nudged a noisy neighbor, and, little by little, the tumult grew less; the angry voices dropped to a lower key, then ceased altogether, and the throng stood still.

Above the murmur, the voice of the singer began to be heard. Then, as the people grew quiet, his notes rang out clear and true. He sang of patriotism, of heroism, of strength in battle. He sang of the deeds of the gods whom the Spartans worshipped. Then, by degrees, his voice grew less ringing; its tones became solemn and soothing. And the people listened; they forgot their anger and discord, and there was a hush over all the great throng.

When he stopped there was silence. Then a voice arose: "The colonists are of our own people. They, too, were Spartans. Shall we send the images to them?"

And a great shout arose, "Yes, yes. Let the images go."

CHAPTER III

FORAGING

The men of Sparta, and the boys from seven years upward, did not eat at home, but at public tables. Their meals were simple, and all fared much the same. Even the kings sat with the citizens and shared the same plain food, which often consisted mainly of black broth and barley bread.

Each citizen of Sparta gave from his own stores a regular quantity of supplies for the tables. He gave barley-meal, wine, cheese, figs, dates, and meat. Extra meat for the tables was sometimes provided by those who went hunting, or from the sacrifices offered at the altars. Then, too, a generous citizen would now and then give white bread, instead of barley bread, or bring birds which he had caught, or offerings of fruit or vegetables when in season.

The food for the boys' tables was simpler and less varied than that for the men's, although plain, simple food was the rule for all.

Very little money was used in Sparta. What they had was of iron. If a man had corn raised upon his land, he exchanged a part of it for other articles which he needed. The market-place of the city was, for this reason, a place of trade, rather than of buying and selling.

After their breakfast, on the morning of the Assembly, Orestes sent the boys of his company away to get food for their table.

"Go where you like outside the city," he said, "but do not return until you can bring something for the common table. Be soldiers now; be men. Stop not for hunger, or pain, or toil, but secure food, and come not back without it.

If you do your work awkwardly and are caught, you will be flogged. Be off."

It was no new message to the boys. This was a part of their training; a part of their education. They were sent out as soldiers to forage for supplies. They might steal, in fact they must steal, but they must not be caught. Therein lay the disgrace. This was a part of their preparation for warfare. It was a national custom, understood by all; and so, although no man wanted his goods stolen,—and he caught and flogged the offender if he could,—he knew that in taking his goods the boys were not breaking the laws of Sparta, but obeying them.

Thus foraging was, to the boys, an exciting game; a chance to test their skill, their dexterity, and often their endurance. And the Spartan boy who could endure most was the hero of his fellows.

"Where shall we go?" asked Brasidas of Chartas, as the company of boys broke up into smaller groups.

"To the mountain!" exclaimed Chartas. "A dish of grapes would taste good at our table, and they must be ripe by this time."

"Just the thing!" replied Brasidas. "A mountain climb suits me, and the grapes will, indeed, be good."

The two boys started westward from the city toward the mountain, with its rocky slopes, its forests, and its snow-crowned peaks. The path they took was rugged, and the climbing steep. But they did not hesitate. The difficulties of the way only made their task more exciting, and would win for them greater credit when they returned.

At first they ran along the path, then they clambered up the side of the mountain. In places the rocks were sharp and broken, and in others there were steep, slippery cliffs, but, although their feet were bare, they climbed the steep places, jumped from one broken rock to another, or pulled themselves up the cliffs by their bare hands.

Suddenly Chartas stopped and threw himself upon a flat rock. Lifting his foot, he pulled from it a large thorn. The blood followed as he did so, but, making no comment, he sped on again after Brasidas.

At last they came to a more open space on the mountain-side. "Now," said Brasidas, "we may begin to look for the vines."

"Yes," said Chartas, "now we must separate and keep hidden."

As he said this he turned to the right and made his way cautiously forward, while Brasidas crept along a cliff to his left.

Suddenly Chartas dropped behind a huge rock. Above him a man, dressed in a leather chiton, was crossing the open space. In his hands he carried large vessels for holding water.

"'Tis one of the slaves who cares for a master's vineyard," said Chartas to himself. He turned his head. Beyond him he saw a grove of plane trees, and, listening intently, he heard the splash of water. "He is going to the fountain in the grove," he said. "The vines are in need of water. They must be near."

He waited until the slave disappeared in the grove, then carefully he made his way upward. It had been a hard climb up the mountain, and his foot ached from the long thorn which had been pulled away, but his one thought was to find the vines, secure the grapes, and make his escape unseen.

He darted forward, now stopping to crouch behind a rock, or to stand close against a tree, while he peered out or listened. Again he darted on; he had seen the vines; they were heavy with purple grapes.

Casting himself among them, he began pulling the clusters. An empty water jar stood near, and hastily he tossed the ripe clusters into it. It was nearly full. He stopped again to listen.

In the distance he heard a slight crackling. It was the sound of footsteps in the grove. The slave was doubtless returning.

Catching up the water jar, he ran farther up the mountain, turned to his right, and stopped again to listen. He could hear the slave, now below him, returning to his vines. Making a circuit, Chartas ran quickly but softly down through the farther side of the grove, and was once more upon the rocky pass which he and Brasidas had climbed.

He stopped for a moment to adjust his jar, for it was large and awkward to carry. At the same moment he heard a shout, then a crashing above him. One thought passed through his mind. The slave had discovered the loss of the jar, and was looking for him. Just an instant he listened again. The sound was coming nearer.

Like some wild animal of the mountains, Chartas turned and jumped. With his bare feet he leaped from jagged rock to jagged rock, holding tightly to his jar, and balancing himself, he knew not how.

It was not the fear of losing his longed-for grapes; it was not the fear of being beaten: that did not matter, for the pain of that would pass. It was the fear of a flogging before his mates, and before the men of the city—not the *pain* of the flogging, but the disgrace of *having failed*.

This was the fear that made him plunge, barefooted, over jutting rocks; that made him swing over cliffs with one hand, while he clutched his jar with the other.

At last he reached the top of the little path which stretched away to the plain below, where stood the houses of Sparta.

He stopped to catch his breath. What was that? He still was followed! The footsteps were close behind him!

AT LAST HE REACHED THE TOP OF THE LITTLE PATH.

Once more fear lent wings to his feet, nor did he notice that a trace of blood was left wherever his feet touched the ground. He did not even know that his hands, as well as his feet, were bleeding. He was too much of a Spartan to care for that, if only he did not fail. On he sped, like the wind.

"Chartas, Chartas! What a runner you are! Stop! Let us go on together!"

Chartas turned his head; caught his breath; then dropped upon the ground. It was Brasidas who had chased him down the mountain!

Upon Brasidas' shoulders rested a bag, filled, like his own water jar, with clusters of grapes.

CHAPTER IV

THE PUBLIC TABLES

When the boys of Orestes' company gathered for their evening meal, Gelon alone was missing. Each boy, as he returned, brought with him something for the tables, fruits, vegetables, olive oil, meat, or meal.

The grapes which Chartas and Brasidas brought were placed upon the tables, that of the old men being supplied first, for age was respected in Sparta. No one commented upon the scratched faces and hands of the two boys, nor upon the marks of blood upon his feet and the slight limp of Chartas, but the older men looked at the boys with approval, although they were careful that they should receive no word of spoken praise. Only Orestes, as he met Chartas, threw his arm across his shoulders in a way that meant much to the younger boy. But even he said nothing. The Spartans were men of deeds, not words.

The boys' tables were separate from those of the men, but the smallest boys sat on stools beside their fathers, and were handed their portions of food.

After the meal the men began talking of the Assembly,

which had been held that day, and the boys listened. They spoke of the ambassador; of the singer. They gave their opinions freely, and they asked many questions of each other, and of the boys.

Then one of the men touched the strings of his cithara, and began to sing. Others took up the song, and soon a great chorus of men's voices arose and filled the large room.

Chartas felt a thrill, as he always did at the sound of music. He remembered when he had seen a company of Spartan soldiers march away to battle singing the same song, and he knew that the greatest singers of Sparta had been her bravest men.

The men stopped singing. Suddenly one of them, named Agis, turned and, nodding toward Brasidas, asked, "Who established the Olympian games?"

"Herakles," replied Brasidas promptly.

"What is the sacred truce?" Agis continued, nodding at Theognis.

"The peace which is preserved between all the states of Greece during the games at Olympia," Theognis answered.

"Why does Sparta need no walls?" came a third question, and this time it was directed to Theron; but Theron was not paying attention, and did not even know that he had been spoken to. He was so intent upon teasing a smaller boy—when he should have been listening and learning—that he now had his back toward the speaker.

"Theron, son of Cinadon," said Agis, and at the tone of his

voice Theron started, and turned, "you have shown disrespect to age, and a contempt for knowledge. You may go out and spend the night among the mountains."

Theron rose and instantly left the room. If any among the boys or men thought the punishment severe, they did not show it by word or look, and they probably did not consider it too severe. But Chartas, remembering his flight down the mountainside during the day, wondered how he would have fared had it been dark. "It is good to give attention," he thought, as the door closed upon Theron.

"Why does Sparta need no walls?" The question was repeated, and this time Agis nodded to Chartas.

"The men of Sparta are her walls," replied Chartas, and the grave men about the tables smiled approvingly at the earnestness of the boy.

Another song was sung, joking remarks were exchanged between the men, some of the boys were quizzed until they scarcely knew how to answer; and then, one by one, the men arose and bade each other good night. There were no lights in the streets, and the streets themselves were irregular and unpaved. The buildings of the city were set here and there without plan, and the streets wound here and there between them. None of the younger men carried lights, but the men who were over sixty were carefully lighted to their homes.

Even the smaller boys of Sparta were accustomed to going about without lights. But none of the boys went home at night. From the time they were seven years old, they slept, as well as ate, in the public buildings which were furnished for that purpose, and each company of boys had its own quarters.

"Gelon has not yet returned," said Theognis, as the boys of Orestes' company gathered in their quarters.

"And now Theron is gone, too," added Brasidas with a shrug of his shoulders.

"To sleep, boys," was the only response of their iren, and at once the boys dropped upon their beds of reeds.

"I wonder if Orestes will suffer for Theron's conduct," wondered Chartas, as he tossed about, for he well knew that the irens were held responsible for the conduct of the boys of their company.

Chartas' muscles were lame and sore, and the bed of rushes was far from soft, but it was the only sort of bed he knew, and he was trained to hardy endurance. It was not long before he was sound asleep.

In the meantime Theron had been following the path to the mountain, over which Chartas and Brasidas had traveled during the day. He might easily have hidden in the dark and irregular streets of the city until morning—but he had been told to go to the mountains. He might, through his love of mischief, be inattentive, but he would scorn to disobey. Besides, there were real dangers in the mountains at night, and to stay in the city would be cowardly, as well as disobedient—and what Spartan boy could bear the brand of cowardice?

So Theron climbed the path till he came to the steeper cliffs. "I will rest on one of these cliffs," he said. "It is safer here than higher up among the trees." Unconsciously he had spoken his thoughts aloud, and as he stopped, he heard an answering sound. He was alert at once. It might be one of the beasts of the mountain, for he well knew that it was the haunt of wild animals, and that they roamed about at night.

He held his breath and listened.

At a little distance he again heard the sound, and then the words, softly spoken, "Can it be you, Theron?"

"Yes," said Theron with a ring of gladness in his voice. "Where are you, Gelon? What has happened?"

"I thought it was your voice," said Gelon, making his way to the cliff. "How came you here? Did you fail, too?"

"No," answered Theron, "I did not fail, for I carried a large cruse of oil to the tables. But yet I am in disgrace." Then he explained how he came to be sent to the mountain.

"And what of you?" he asked, in conclusion.

"Oh, I am due to have a flogging," said Gelon, reluctantly. "Not that I mind *that*, but I stole a piece of meat and was making off with it, when I caught my foot in a vine and stumbled. I fell headlong, and scared a flock of sheep, who ran bleating in all directions. That called out their owner, and he saw me. I got away without being caught, but the piece of meat flew from my arms when I fell, and dropped to a great distance below me, for I was on a steep hillside. The man was upon me too soon for me to get it again, and I would not go back to barracks empty-handed."

"So you have stayed here in the mountain!" exclaimed Theron. "I am glad that I came this way. As soon as it is light, we will forage again, and perhaps we can both find food for the tables."

"That is good of you," said Gelon. He had been without food since morning, but he added, "I shall not go back till I succeed."

CHAPTER V

CHARTAS' HOME

The boys were awakened the next morning by the voice of Orestes.

"Up, boys," he called. "Throw out the reeds. After our morning meal you are to gather fresh material for beds."

It did not take the boys long to carry out Orestes' command, for there was no time spent in dressing and undressing among the boys of Sparta. They hastily gathered up the reeds upon which they had slept, and soon were back with hearty appetites.

There were no dainties set before them, but they had plenty of coarse, plain food, and after they had finished the meal they raced down to the river bank. They then followed the stream until it broadened out over a marsh. Here the reeds grew thickly, and the boys were soon wading in the water and pulling great armfuls of them, for these were the only beds they were allowed. In the winter they gathered down from thistles, and with this down made their beds softer and warmer. But this was the only difference, although the winters were cold. If a boy pulled too much down for his bed, he was ridiculed by the others.

"I wonder how it fares with Theron," said Chartas, as he bent to pull another bunch of reeds.

"And with Gelon," added Brasidas.

Although the boys of Sparta were taught to be hardy, and to despise a lack of courage in any of their number, yet the fifteen boys who made up each company were bound together very closely by their constant association.

Nearly all the boys of Orestes' company had homes and parents in the city, but as we have learned, after a boy reached the age of seven, he became a son of the State, and his education and training were in charge of the State. He no longer lived at the home of his parents.

"I wonder what adventures they are having," Chartas said a moment later, as he returned for another armful of reeds. He had scarcely finished speaking when he heard a shout, and, looking up, he discovered Gelon and Theron running down the river bank.

"Here they are," exclaimed Brasidas, "and together! And look, look! They are carrying a young pig between them!"

"It is squealing yet," laughed Chartas. "How did they ever manage to get away with that? Well," he added, "one thing is certain. The pig will save them from a flogging!"

Later that day, when the boys had had their daily swim in the river and had practised at the gymnasium, those who wished to do so were allowed to visit their homes.

Chartas and Theognis started off together, for their homes were in the same part of the city.

"'Twill soon be time for the festival," said Theognis.

"Yes," replied Chartas, "and I suppose my sister is practising for the dances."

"And mine, too," responded Theognis, as he ran on, for Chartas had reached his home.

The house of Danaus, the father of Chartas, was a large but plain building, with an outer court which was separated from the street by a wall. Inside this court stood a rude image of the god Apollo, who was believed by the Spartans to protect and bless all who entered the house.

As Chartas passed the image, he laid before it a cluster of flowers which he had picked for an offering. As he did so he murmured, "Grant to me, oh, Apollo, that which is honorable and good." He then pushed open the door of the house and entered.

The door of this, as of all the houses of Sparta, was roughly made. It had been sawed from boards, without other finish. The ceilings were hewed with an axe. Only the temples and public buildings of Sparta could be beautifully finished and ornamented. Lycurgus, who had given the city its laws, wanted the people to love simplicity.

As Chartas entered the house, he heard the sound of merry shouts and laughter, and saw his father prancing about astride a stick, while his younger brother and sister ran after, clapping their hands and trying to imitate his steps.

Chartas laughed, too, and he wondered whether the other

men of Sparta, who seemed—as his father did—so quiet and grave in the Assembly and at the public tables, ever played with their children like this.

"Ah, Chartas, my son!"

Chartas turned as he heard the words, for he knew that it was his mother's voice, and then she threw her arms about him.

The children stopped their play to greet him, and soon he was recounting, to them all, the adventures of his company. They laughed heartily when he told them how Brasidas had chased him down the mountain.

"But you held to your jar of grapes!" his mother, Helen, exclaimed.

"Yes, Mother," answered Chartas.

"That was best of all," said his mother, and the eyes of Danaus shone, too, with approval, for they saw that Chartas had shown the hardihood and endurance which were the traits most admired in a Spartan boy.

Then he told them about Theron and Gelon, and of how they had returned after their night in the mountain, carrying the squealing pig. This story, too, was received with hearty laughter.

As Chartas finished his story, the door again opened, and a beautiful young girl entered. It was Melissa, the older sister of Chartas.

"Ah, Chartas!" she exclaimed, "I am glad to see you at home. We so seldom see you now.

"It seems good to be at home," said Chartas. "And where have you been?"

"I have just come from the gymnasium," answered Melissa. "We have been practising the dances for the festival, and, oh, Chartas!" she added, "I am learning to play well upon the lyre."

"Let me hear you play," said Chartas eagerly.

Melissa brought her lyre and played as she sang, and presently they all joined their voices with hers, even the children singing with the rest.

"I am sorry," said Chartas, when the song was ended, "but I must go back, for it will not do to be late. Orestes is such a splendid captain, I would not want him blamed for any fault of mine."

"I will go with you," said Danaus, rising. "It will soon be time for our evening meal. Perhaps," he added with a smile, "we may have a bit of pork for our supper!"

As they were walking along the street, Chartas pointed to an image that stood near a temple. "Why is that image placed there?" he asked.

"I cannot tell you *why*," Danaus replied, "but I suppose you know that it represents the God of Laughter. We Spartans are considered a grave and severe people, and so, in a way, we are. But, so far as I know, we are the only people who have ever erected a statue to the God of Laughter."

MELISSA BROUGHT HER LYRE AND PLAYED AS SHE SANG.

CHAPTER VI

SPARTA'S LAWS

After Danaus and Chartas had left the house, Helen, the wife of Danaus, Melissa, and the younger children, ate their evening meal together. They were waited upon by the household slaves.

"When I am seven, I will go with Father and Chartas to the public tables," said the younger brother proudly.

"Yes," replied his mother, "in two years more you will become a son of the State. Then you will have no mother and no slaves to wait upon you. But you will learn how to endure hard things, and you will become a true Spartan of whom Mother will be proud." She laid her hand upon his head as she spoke.

"I am a Spartan now," said the boy, drawing himself up very straight.

"Yes," replied his mother, smiling, "but not a very big one."

"Melissa," said the little fellow after their meal was finished, "I wish you would tell me a story."

"What sort of a story do you want to hear?" asked Melissa with a smile.

"Oh—about the Law-Giver of Sparta!" exclaimed the boy with shining eyes.

"What do *you* know about the 'Law-Giver of Sparta?'" laughed Melissa.

"Oh, I know; I heard Father telling about him one day," said the boy, with a wise shake of his head. "Some day," he added, "I shall learn the laws, as Chartas does, and I want to hear the story of Ly—Ly—what was his name, Melissa?"

"Lycurgus," said Melissa, as she put her arm about the sturdy little fellow. "Lycurgus was a very wise man," she went on, "and he lived a great many years ago. He loved Sparta, and he wanted her people to be wise and happy. So he thought a great deal, and he studied a great deal, and at last he made a set of laws which he believed would make the Spartans a strong, hardy, happy people.

"He wanted to be very sure that his laws were good, so he went to Delphi, and asked the oracle at Delphi about them.

"The oracle told him that his laws were the best in all the world.

"So Lycurgus taught his laws to the people, and the Spartans kept the laws.

"But Lycurgus was afraid that after he died the people might forget his laws, or try to have them changed, so, after a long time, when he grew to be an old man, he told the Spartans that he was going again to Delphi, and he had the people promise that they would keep his laws until he came back.

"The people made a solemn promise that they would do this."

"And he didn't come back, did he?" interrupted the boy eagerly. "I remember; Father said so."

"No," answered Melissa, "he never came back; and so, after all these years, his laws are still kept—for the people promised, you know."

"Yes, I know," nodded the boy earnestly. "Thank you, Melissa. That was a good story."

The laws of Lycurgus, of which Melissa had told, were different from those of any other country. They provided that each Spartan should be given a certain amount of land, and slaves to take care of it. The Spartans were to spend their time in public affairs, such as the military and religious festivals, the education of the children, and the enforcement of the laws.

They did not carry on trade with other countries, or engage in the manufacture even of such articles as they themselves used. This was done by a class of men who had been conquered by the Spartans in battle, and who occupied a position between that of the Spartans and the slaves, who were called Helots.

All lines of work were passed on from father to son. A flute player was sure to be the son of a flute player; a maker of drinking-cups was sure to be the son of a man who had made drinking-cups. Even the cooks who made the black broth which appeared so often upon Spartan tables, had learned to make it from their fathers, and these men in turn, from their fathers before them.

Customs did not change in Sparta. Lycurgus had not intended that they should.

That evening, as Chartas and Theognis were on their way to quarters, Chartas suddenly asked, "Had you heard that Cinadon was on trial to-day before the ephors?"

"No," replied Theognis. "What was his offence?"

"He was accused of bringing a quantity of silver money into Sparta."

"And was he found guilty?" asked Theognis.

"Yes," replied Chartas, with a laugh. "He was found guilty and ordered to go without his dessert at table for ten days, as punishment."

Theognis, too, laughed, although a fine of this sort was not unusual in Sparta.

"Hurry, you are late," called Brasidas, who was standing at the door of their quarters, and Chartas and Theognis hastened their steps.

They were just in time to take their places for the drill upon the laws, which every Spartan boy was expected to learn.

Soon, in unison with the others, they began to chant—half singing, half reciting—and beating time to the rhythm with their bare feet:

> "When ye have builded a temple to Zeus,
>   To Syllarian Zeus and Syllarian Athena,
>   Divided the folk into tribes and clans,
>   And established a Senate of thirty persons,

Including the two Kings,
Ye shall summon the folk to a stated Assembly
And these shall have the deciding voice."

And thus the laws of Lycurgus were taught from one generation to another.

CHAPTER VII

THE FESTIVAL

The day of the festival had arrived, and the boys of the city were released from their usual drills and exercises.

There were no school buildings in Sparta. The boys were taught in the gymnasium or the barracks. They learned a little reading, a little writing, and a very little arithmetic. But greater attention was given to teaching them the laws; in training them to speak well in public; to recite the great poems of Homer; and to sing the national songs, and accompany them with the cithara. Then, too, they were taught to exercise, to swim, run, wrestle, ride, play football, and throw the discus. In spite of the hardihood of the Spartans, the rougher sports of that time were forbidden.

The girls of Sparta were given much the same training as the boys, although they were trained separately, and their leaders were young women. Unlike the girls of Athens, they were allowed to go freely upon the streets, and to join in the choruses and festivals. Only the married women of Sparta wore veils upon their faces when outside their homes. The Spartan girls played upon the lyre instead of the cithara.

The most beautiful women of all Greece were those of Sparta, for their outdoor life and athletic exercises gave them clear skins, bright eyes, and graceful, healthful bodies.

The day of the festival had arrived, and the boys and girls of the city were released from their usual drills and exercises.

The festival began with a procession, and the boys of Orestes' company took their places. First came the kings, who were to offer sacrifices to the gods; next the magistrates; and after these, the men of the city, the companies of maidens, and the companies of boys. Some of the men rode horses, and some of the maidens were in chariots, or in beautifully ornamented cars. They drove their horses quite as fearlessly as the men.

As the procession moved through the streets, the people sang a song, or paean, in thanksgiving for the bountiful harvests of the year. They stepped lightly, in time with the music, for their hearts were as joyous as those of children.

They reached the temple, and here the priests offered a sacrifice, and poured wine upon the altar.

As the people formed in groups, here and there, Orestes and Chartas stood together, near the other boys of their company.

"Did you notice how well Theognis sang the paean?" asked Chartas.

"Yes," replied Orestes. "There is something unusual about Theognis. He loves poetry, and music, and the graceful exercises of the gymnasium. It is my belief that he will some day be a poet, himself."

"Theognis a poet!" exclaimed Chartas, in surprise. And then he added: "There is something different about him—perhaps that is it!!"

"But see!" said Orestes.

A chorus of singers had joined hands, and were now dancing slowly about the blazing altar, and, as they sang, several of the men of Sparta acted in pantomime the words of the song.

Then a group of maidens came forward and danced with measured steps and graceful gestures, while one of their number played upon the lyre.

"See," said Chartas to Orestes, "my sister, Melissa, is among the dancers."

"Yes," answered Orestes, "she dances well." And Chartas noted with pleasure that Orestes' eyes followed her graceful figure throughout the dance.

"Now for the war dance!" exclaimed Chartas. "I think that is best of all."

A group of men took their places before the assembly. A flute player stood among them. There was silence for a moment, then he put his flute to his lips. Quickly and lightly the men began to dance, and, in perfect time to the music, they imitated the actions of a soldier in battle. They assumed an attitude of defence,—crouching, and presenting their shields; they avoided the thrust of an enemy; they sprang up; retreated; then sprang forward to thrust with their short swords; backward to throw a lance; and upright to draw a bow.

The people watched with breathless interest, for this, the Pyrrhic war dance, was best liked of all their dances.

"Isn't it wonderful how well they can do i t!" exclaimed Chartas.

"Yes," said Orestes, "but I shall expect you to do it as well some day."

"I?" questioned Chartas in astonishment.

"You!" answered Orestes with a quiet smile. "I am to teach it to our company very soon, and I will take special pains to drill you in it, if you wish."

"Oh, I do!" exclaimed Chartas, "and I will try my best. I would rather dance the Pyrrhic ajar dance well, than take any other part in the festivals."

"Very well, then," replied Orestes. "You shall be given the chance."

Chartas' eyes were shining with pleasure as Orestes said, "Come, it is our turn now."

Three groups were formed. One was of old men; the next was of the active men of the city; the third was of boys—the boys of Orestes' and Procles' companies.

The old men sang:

"We once were young and brave and strong.

The next group responded:

"And we're so now, come on and try."

Then the boys sang:

"But we'll be strongest by and by."

As the boys sang, Chartas again noticed how the voice of Theognis led all the others.

After the procession and dances, there was a great feast. Chartas had told the boys of his company that they were to be taught the Pyrrhic war dance, and it was the chief topic of conversation while they feasted.

"Good!" Brasidas exclaimed. "That is the dance for Spartans."

And Theognis echoed his exclamation. "Nothing else has such perfect rhythm of motion," he added.

Later in the day there were gymnastic exercises, and the great festival day closed with chariot races between men, and others between girls.

"See how well Gorgo handles her horses," exclaimed Brasidas, as one of the chariots swept past him.

"Yes," replied Theron, who was beside him,

"she handles them quite as well as any man." "That is what Spartan training does for our girls!" proudly exclaimed an older man who had overheard them. "In no other country are the girls so graceful and so strong."

CHAPTER VIII

WORK AND PLAY

The festival was the one topic of conversation among the boys of Sparta during the days that followed. Naturally, they were most interested in the Pyrrhic war dance, and the chariot races. The boys of Orestes' company were eagerly discussing the news that Chartas had brought them.

"Did you say that *we* were to be taught the Pyrrhic dance?" asked Gelon, with shining eyes, as he pushed forward among the boys.

"Yes," answered Chartas, "so Orestes told me at the festival."

"I wonder when we are to begin," said Theognis, eagerly.

"Soon, I think," Chartas replied.

"I wish it were to-day!" exclaimed Theron.

"Well, it will not be to-day," said the hearty voice of Orestes, who had come upon the group unnoticed, "so be off to your tasks. Chartas, Brasidas, Theognis, and Gelon are to bring wood for the fires. The rest of you," he added, with a wave of his hand, "are to gather vegetables and greens for the tables."

The boys scattered at once: the four older boys to the woods; while the younger boys, led by Theron, slipped away to the country outside Sparta. Stealthily, and unseen, they crept here and there into gardens and fields, and gathered such supplies of vegetables as they could carry away unseen.

"My!" sputtered Ceos, a boy of lively tongue, as he overtook Theron later on. "I thought I was going to lose my skin that time. I came near getting caught, for the old slave who was after me was very light of foot. Why do they care so much," he added, "when they know that the State makes us steal for the tables?"

"Because they have worked to raise the stuff, I suppose," said Theron laughingly.

"Yes," answered Ceos, "but it is the State that provides them the land to raise it on. They do not own the land."

"That is so," replied Theron, "and I suppose that is what gives the State the right to send us out foraging upon their lands. All property really belongs to the State."

"Yes," replied Ceos, "that is the way my father explained it to me. He says, too, that soldiers, when marching or in camp, have to secure their food by foraging, or starve. It is the duty of the State to train us for soldiers."

"The girls are never sent to forage," said Theron.

"They could do it!" responded Ceos.

"Yes, they are as quick as we are," assented Theron, "but they do not go to war."

Suddenly the two boys stopped. Placing upon the ground their gifts for the tables, they stood erect, their arms folded across their breasts, and their eyes cast down.

An old man with white hair and long white beard passed them. He was one of the senators; and every citizen of Sparta paid to the senators a reverence which even their Kings might envy.

After their long tramp of the morning, the boys were put through their exercises and drills in the gymnasium, and later they were given a short time in which to amuse themselves as they pleased.

"Let us have a play," called out Theognis.

"A play! a play!" the other boys responded, and away they raced to the open space just below the city.

"'What shall it be?" asked Gelon, as they stopped for breath.

"The fruit stealers," suggested Theron.

."That is good; that is good!" cried the others,

"Who will take the parts?" asked Brasidas. "Who will be thief?"

None of the boys responded.

"Well, I will be then," said Brasidas. "Now, who will be the owner of the fruit?"

"I will take that," said Ceos laughingly. "I saw, this morning, a fine example of the way that should be played."

"Did you get caught?" cried Gelon.

"No," answered Ceos, "but I can imagine the flogging. I have seen it acted at other times," he added with a grim smile, at which all the boys laughed.

After a few other details had been arranged, the play began.

"AN OLD MAN WITH WHITE HAIR AND LONG WHITE
BEARD…"

Ceos pretended to be busily at work among his fruit-trees. Brasidas came running from a distance; then he stopped, and began slowly and cautiously to creep up to the trees. Finally he pretended to begin picking the fruit. At first he watched the owner of the trees, as he worked; then, becoming eager to gather the fruit, he became less watchful.

During the progress of the play, the other boys looked on, occasionally imitating the actions of the two boys taking part, by a light, rhythmic motion that was almost a dance.

Suddenly Ceos seemed to catch sight of the thief. Quickly but quietly he ran toward Brasidas, and had almost reached him when Brasidas looked up.

Grasping, apparently, his fruit, Brasidas darted away, Ceos but a few feet behind.

"Brasidas' longer legs will save him!" shouted Chartas.

"He will win the race!" exclaimed Theognis.

"Ceos is smaller," said Theron, "but he is quick. See, he is holding his own!"

"Good!" shouted the boys, clapping their hands. "Ceos is plucky."

But Ceos' legs were shorter, and the distance between the two began to increase, when suddenly Brasidas, in glancing back at his pursuer, struck his foot upon a projecting rock. His arms, in which he had pretended to be holding his fruit, flew wide, and he fell headlong upon the ground.

In an instant Ceos was upon him, and with his hard little

Spartan fists he began beating Brasidas with a right good will. Then, jumping to his feet, he pretended to pick up the scattered fruit.

The boys shouted and cheered. The play was over.

"That was well done," said Gelon.

"You are a good runner, Ceos," said Brasidas heartily, as they made their way back to the city. "Why don't you train for the footrace at the games?"

"I am afraid you would compete," replied Ceos, "and there are no stones on the course at Olympia."

CHAPTER IX

NEW ADVENTURES

Every household in Sparta had its slaves. These slaves, or Helots, had been conquered in battle, and for all the succeeding years they were slaves to the Spartans. They could not be sold, as the slaves of Athens could, neither could they be freed, for, in a way, they were considered the property of the State.

As we have learned, no Spartan citizen took part in any manual labor, nor even engaged in business. His time was spent in the gymnasium, practising military and athletic exercises; in hunting; in the management of public affairs; and in religious ceremonies and festivals. He regarded freedom from labor as freedom from pain—as complete liberty. Yet the Spartans were by no means indolent, and a lazy man was severely punished, and held in contempt.

Sparta's laws were not written laws. It was said that they were "written in the hearts of her citizens," and they were administered by the senators. The laws provided that a certain number of slaves were to be allowed to each Spartan, and so the slaves cultivated the farm lands belonging to the citizens, and carried on the household duties in the homes of the city.

Now, even the slaves of Sparta had caught, from the festival, the desire to play.

"Come, Chartas," said Gelon quietly, as he met him in the street, late in the day. "There is fun in store for us. Come."

"What is going on?" asked Chartas, following.

"The slaves of some of the neighboring households are about to give a play. I have found a place where we can watch without their seeing us. Hurry!"

"Wait," said Chartas. "There go Brasidas and Ceos. I will call them."

"But be quick," said Gelon anxiously.

A moment later, the four boys, hidden from the sight of the slaves, were eagerly watching the strange sight.

The play of the slaves could hardly be called a play; it was, rather, a wild and extravagant dance, without rhythm or beauty; and yet, in a rude way, they imitated various actions and occupations of men. Some of the imitations were funny, while others were simply awkward and common.

"See!" said Chartas, touching Brasidas' arm. "Watch the slave yonder. He has been drinking too much. He can scarcely keep upon his feet. Yet he is still trying to dance."

"See him stagger!" said Brasidas. "He will fall yet."

The interest of all four of the boys was now centered upon the drunken Helot.

As they looked, the man almost lost his balance, and tumbled against another of the company. This man turned quickly and struck him.

"See his face," said Brasidas, "how stupid he looks."

"And how foolish he acts," added Ceos.

"Bah!" exclaimed Chartas, "it is no wonder the men of Sparta think it a disgrace to become drunk."

"Look again!" said Gelon. "He has fallen."

It was true. The man lay stupidly upon the ground, making no effort to rise again. The rest of the company danced on, for most of them had been drinking, and their steps, too, were beginning to be unsteady, and their faces bloated and stupid, while some were growing quarrelsome.

"What a sight!" exclaimed Chartas, as he turned away. "It seems strange that wine can turn men into such beasts as that!"

"'Tis a good thing to know that it does," said Gelon.

"Yes," responded Chartas, "it *is* a good thing. I am glad that Spartans are taught to despise drunkenness.

"Ah, here is Orestes," he cried, as they started down the street, and, darting forward, he was soon at the side of his captain.

"Well!" exclaimed Orestes, "where did you come from so suddenly?"

"Oh," answered Chartas, "we boys have been watching the Helots give one of their plays. But it was disgusting, for they became drunk at the last, and acted like beasts."

"'Tis good that you saw it!" exclaimed Orestes. "Drunkenness surely does make men like animals, or worse, for it stupefies the brain."

"Hark! Do you hear the music?" asked Brasidas suddenly, for the other boys had also overtaken their captain.

"Listen!" said Orestes.

The boys stood still for a moment.

"It is a cithara," said Orestes, "but different. I cannot make out what the difference is."

"Let us see who is playing," suggested Ceos. So, together they hurried down the street.

It was not long before they came in sight of a great crowd of boys, and in their midst was the musician. Among the crowd were the other boys of their company—in fact it soon seemed as though all the boys and youths of Sparta had been drawn to the spot by the music.

The player kept on, gratified by the attention which he was receiving. His music, as Orestes had said, was different from that usually heard in Sparta. Its harmonies were fuller, stronger, and yet there was a soft, tender cadence which was strangely in contrast to the music of Sparta.

"I have it!" exclaimed Orestes at length, turning to Chartas. "See! We have seven strings on our citharas: his has nine. That is what gives the fuller harmonies."

"Yes, but still 'tis different," returned Chartas. "It is not the music of the paeans; 'tis softer, more quiet."

"You are right," said Orestes. "I should say it was more the music of Athens than of Sparta."

He had scarcely finished speaking when a strong voice commanded the musician to stop, and strong hands sent the crowd of boys scattering in all directions.

"Stop!" said the voice—and Orestes saw that it was one of the ephors of the city speaking. "Cut from your instrument its added strings! You are not to poison the ears of our youth by the music of a luxury-loving people. The Spartans are not of such! Our music is free, bold, inspiring. We will keep it so!"

Abashed, the musician placed his instrument in the out-stretched hand of the ephor, who cut from it the added strings, while the boys who had listened sped away to their quarters, and dropped—still half-frightened at the anger in the ephor's voice–upon their hard little beds.

CHAPTER X

A VACANCY FILLED

The next few days were days of intense excitement for the boys. They were preparing for the war game in which two companies of Spartan boys took part each year. It had been announced that the companies of Orestes and Procles had been chosen for the conflict. In no other state than Sparta would this have been called a game.

Early upon the day appointed, a sacrifice was made upon one of the altars, and then the two companies of boys, to the music of the cithara and the fife, marched away from the city to an island which had been made ready for them. This island was formed by ditches filled with water, and it was reached by two bridges upon opposite sides. One was called the bridge of Herakles, and was guarded by an image of this hero-god. The other was the bridge of Lycurgus, with its image of Sparta's great law-giver. Orestes' company crossed the bridge of Herakles; Procles' company the bridge of Lycurgus, and, facing each other, they stood, quivering with excitement; eager to show their courage and endurance.

The citizens and boys of Sparta had followed the two companies, and now surrounded the island, intent upon the out-come of the conflict.

The struggle began by wrestling, but as one opponent or an-other was thrown, a fury seemed to seize the boys. It was no longer a wrestling contest; it became a hand-to-hand struggle; a war of strength and physical endurance.

We, of to-day, can scarcely understand how such a contest among boys could have received the approval of sober-minded men; but the Spartans despised pain and honored physical hardihood. That they should have given so great a degree of honor to mere physical courage, is the chief reproach that has been brought against the Spartans. The moral, as well as physi-cal, courage which made them die in battle rather than let a for-eign army take possession of their lands and their homes, was altogether different from this.

When Orestes, with his victorious company of boys, marched back to the city, they bore grim evidence of their sturdy fighting in the war game which Spartan custom en-dorsed;—but Ceos, with his ready fun, was not with them, nor would he be again.

The older men, however, as they marched back to the city, said tersely, "The best survive."

The days that followed were filled as usual, for the boys, with exercises in the gymnasium; with tasks which took them to the mountains, to the river, and out into the farming country; and with lessons in music and the study of Homer.

The poems of Homer—the Iliad and the Odyssey—stirred the enthusiasm of the boys, not only because they told of wars and strange adventures, but because Helen, of whom the Iliad told, was stolen away from Sparta, and from her husband, Menelaus, who was one of Sparta's early kings.

The lessons in singing were of great importance. The boys were not taught to sing alone, so much as in chorus. They were trained by one of the older men of the city under the superintendence of an ephor, or magistrate.

Every festival had its chorus of singers, and there were many festivals. At the games and processions there were choruses, and in every battle the Spartan warriors advanced singing.

So the boys, and also the girls, of Sparta, were taught to sing, and the singing was accompanied by the cithara, the lyre, or the flute.

The character of the music was in keeping with that of the people. It was severe, and yet had a simple grandeur which inspired the singers as well as the hearers.

"Who was Terpander?" asked the singing-master, suddenly, during one of his lessons. He addressed his question to Chartas.

"A great Spartan musician," answered Chartas. "He invented the seven-stringed lyre."

"What else did he do?" questioned the master of Theognis.

"He won four prizes for his music at the Pythian games," replied Theognis. "And he once quieted a tumult in the city, by his playing,—as was done at the last meeting of the Assembly," Theognis added, with shining eyes.

"Good," said the master. Then, turning to Gelon, he asked: "How many strings had the lyre before Terpander?"

"But two," answered Gelon.

"I wonder if the master is thinking of the musician we heard a few days ago," said Theron to Brasidas. "I wonder if *he* thought himself a second Terpander!"

The master raised his hand; the room grew silent. Then there burst forth the stirring strains of a Spartan war song, and the boys sang with a will:

> "Now fight we for our children, for this land;
> Our lives unheeding, let us bravely die.
> Courage, ye youths! together firmly stand;
> Think not of fear, nor ever turn to fly."

At the close of the lesson, Orestes addressed the boys of his company:

"Our company now numbers but fourteen," he said, gravely. "Penthilus, son of Androcles, has been mentioned to fill our ranks. What have you to say?"

As Orestes asked the question, Theognis stepped forth. "I have seen Penthilus show disrespect for age. I should not like to have him one of our number," he said, and stepped back to his place.

"As you know," said Orestes, "no one is admitted into a company who is not approved by all. I have another name: Dorus, son of Cleomenes."

Chartas turned to Brasidas. "'Tis the king's youngest son."

"I know him," said Brasidas. "He is small of stature, but strong and active."

"He already rides the swiftest horse in the king's stables," commented Theron.

"I have heard of him as a fearless hunter," added Gelon.

"Will he give and take with the rest, or will he be the king's son?" asked another of the boys.

"He will give and take," cried Brasidas. "Have no fear as to that."

"Are any dissatisfied with the choice Dorus, son of Cleomenes?" asked Orestes.

There was silence.

"He is one of us," said Orestes,—and Ceos' place was filled.

That night, while the boys of his company slept, Orestes paced back and forth outside the barracks, his mind upon the war game in which his company had taken part. His face was set; his hands were clenched.

"'Tis a custom unworthy of Sparta!" he exclaimed bitterly. "'Tis a waste of life, for which there is no reasonable excuse! But Sparta requires it, and not even to Chartas may I show my grief!"

CHAPTER XI

A PLEDGE AND A CHASE

"The election occurs to-day," said Orestes, as he and Chartas came back together from their morning bath in the Eurotas.

"I knew of the death of the senator," replied Chartas. "Who is likely to be elected in his place?"

"Two men have offered themselves," answered Orestes. "One is Laertes; the other Diodorus. Both are men of blameless lives and upright character. They belong to distinguished families, and have spent their sixty years of life in the service of Sparta. It seems to me that it will be a close contest between them."

"But you will vote," said Chartas. "Who is your choice?"

"I shall vote for Laertes," said Orestes decisively.

"And what is your reason?" asked Chartas.

"The records of the two men are equally honorable," responded Orestes, "but since the laws of Sparta are unwritten, and must be delivered by the senators, it seems to me that the man of good judgment, who is thoughtful, and of an open mind, is the man to choose. I believe Laertes to be such a man. He is not easily swayed by passion; he has wonderful self-control."

Orestes' words showed that he had weighed the matter carefully and well, and Chartas was impressed by the fact.

"Chartas," he added earnestly, throwing his arm across the boy's shoulder with the familiar gesture which always awakened a deeper love and loyalty upon Chartas' part, "let us pledge ourselves to a worthy purpose: let us keep our lives so open and honorable that—if it is not the will of the gods that we die in battle—we may be deserving of a place among her most honored men."

Chartas was deeply touched. He knew that among all the captains of the city, none was more honored by the older men, nor more admired by the boys of the city, than Orestes. And he had been both proud and happy that he had been chosen as Orestes' special friend. Now he realized, more fully than ever, what this friendship meant to him.

"He is more than brave," he thought. "He is honored even now, young as he is, because he is *morally* brave. If he lives, *he* will some day be a senator." He looked up into Orestes' face, and, as he met the eyes of his captain, his own shone with an answering purpose. He slipped his hand into that of his friend, and, with a new resolve, walked with him hack to their barracks.

Later in the day, as the boys began climbing one of the mountain paths outside the city, they heard a great shout, as though a multitude of men were calling out.

They stopped.

"It is the Assembly voting," said Chartas. "I wonder who will be elected."

"How they shout!" exclaimed Brasidas. "I always want to shout, too, when I hear the men. But come, we were sent out to hunt, and we must not go back empty-handed."

"Shall we scatter, or hunt together?" asked Dorus, but before any one could reply there was a quick exclamation from Theron.

The boys looked. At a little distance they saw a young fox, about half grown, trotting along through a bit of forest.

Without a word, the boys bounded forward. At the same moment, the fox discovered the boys. The chase was an exciting one. The fox, used to the rocks and ledges, as well as to the forest, ran surely and swiftly. But the hardy, barefoot boys were scarcely less sure of foot, and they, too, were good runners.

Perhaps, in a more equal chase, the fox might have outstripped them, but with more than a dozen boys in full pursuit, it is no wonder that it became confused, turned in its course, and, in so doing, ran across the path of Chartas.

Chartas sprang forward, dropped, and buried his two hands deep in the long fur of the animal.

The struggle that followed was fierce and exciting. The boys stood about and watched, ready to help if Chartas asked it. But they understood too well the Spartan code of honor to interfere unasked.

The fighters were well matched for strength, the boy and the fox. Chartas had only his bare hands for weapons, while the fox fought with teeth and claws. But Chartas' hands were strong, his muscles hard, and back of them were a fierce courage and a wonderful power of endurance.

The fox bit at his bare arms, and his legs. It scratched and tore his flesh, but slowly Chartas' hands were working forward, while his tense muscles held the frantic animal with an unyielding hold. At last his hands reached the throat. With all the strength of his hardened muscles, Chartas tightened his grip. The fox gave one spasmodic twist, and its struggle was ended.

Then the boys shouted! Again and again the forest rang with their cries of "Chartas! Chartas!" and of "Victor! Victor!"

When their first excitement had subsided they pressed about him, praising him, and exclaiming over his deed.

"Good!" cried Gelon. "That was far better than the story we are told by our masters, of the brave boy who let the fox destroy him. I have always wondered why he did not choke the little beast when he had it so well hidden!"

Amid the laughter that followed Gelon's remark, Brasidas took Chartas' hand. "Come," he said, "let me wash your wounds. A clean wound is soon healed, you know."

So, laughing, praising and shouting, the boys led Chartas to a clear stream that flowed down the mountain, and there, in the cold water, washed the scratched and torn flesh of the sturdy young Spartan.

It was time for the evening meal when Chartas, bearing his trophy upon his back, led the group of boys into their quarters.

Some of the older men half rose to their feet when they saw him, and the face of Danaus lighted with pleasure, for Chartas' burden was all the explanation they needed for his torn and still bleeding flesh. Some of the men openly praised him, and all showed their approval.

He cast the body of the fox upon the floor and, looking up, met the eyes of Orestes. There was no need of words.

"Have your wounds been cleansed?" asked Orestes; and there was a note of personal concern in his voice.

"Yes," replied Chartas. "Brasidas washed them in the stream."

"That is good," said Orestes; and then he added earnestly, "You have borne yourself well!"

CHAPTER XII

THE DRILL

The next morning, after their regular duties, and their plunge in the river, the boys went to the gymnasium. They were making good progress in their practice of the Pyrrhic war dance, and they found it by far the most interesting of their daily drills.

When they were in readiness, the flute player sounded the notes to which the Spartan soldiers led an attack when in battle. The boys were divided for the dance into smaller groups, and, at the sound of the flute, each boy placed upon his head a crown, and grasped his shield. Then, as the stirring notes continued, they advanced by divisions, and went through the evolutions of an army going into battle.

Their step was not the steady marching step of the soldier of to-day. It was, rather, a springing, dancing movement, light, and quick, and graceful. Indeed, the soldiers of Sparta were often spoken of as dancers, even in actual war.

There were many positions for the boys to learn. There was the attitude of defence, and the movement of attack. They must learn to crouch behind their shields; to spring up; to thrust as with a spear. It was splendid exercise for the muscles, and these lithe, sinewy boys tingled with the joy and the exhilaration of the play. But it exercised more than the muscles. It made them alert, quick to hear, quick to think, quick to act.

Chartas was foremost among the boys of his company in the grace of his movements, and the readiness with which he responded to the commands of the leader. But although this was partly due to his own natural aptitude, he owed much to the careful private drill of Orestes.

"You dance well!" exclaimed Dorus, admiringly, as he and Chartas left the gymnasium together.

"But Orestes deserves most of the credit," Chartas answered frankly.

"I know that you are the favorite of Orestes," said Dorus, making the statement in the matter-of-fact manner in which a captain's preference was always accepted, "and, to my mind, you are the most favored boy in Sparta. There is no other captain in the city to compare with Orestes."

"That is true," said Chartas, with shining eyes, for he loved to hear his captain praised. And then he added, "I am glad we have you in our company."

"I was pleased, I can tell you!" exclaimed Dorus, "and so was my father, the king."

"We are to spend the rest of the day outside the city," said Chartas. "Where shall we go."

"I should like to follow the river below Sparta," responded Dorus. "What do you say to that?"

"It suits me," answered Chartas. "Shall we ask Brasidas to join us?"

"Yes," replied Dorus readily. "I like Brasidas. He is a good companion, and a true Spartan."

Both above and below Sparta, the bed of the Eurotas lay between high, hilly lands, and on the west towered the rocky heights of the mountain. Here the stream was swift, and below the city it tumbled over rocks, forming a rapid cascade. But lower down the river broadened out over a level plain. Here grew the reeds and the rushes which the boys were sent to gather for their beds.

To follow the Eurotas was one of the favorite excursions of the boys.

Several miles below Sparta, there were the ruins of ancient temples and statues, and a vaulted underground cemetery.

The three boys ran races, climbed over rocks, or forded the river, as the impulse directed them. Occasionally they sat down to watch the water, or to talk.

"I wonder what gave the river its name," said Brasidas, as they sat watching the swift eddies between some great rocks.

"Don't you know?" asked Dorus. "'Tis named for Eurotas, son of Myles. The water used to rise and overflow the level plain below us, destroying the crops. Eurotas had a canal dug to keep the river in its bed. That was a great many years ago, but the stream was named in his honor."

"'Tis well you told us the story," said Chartas. "Some of the men might have asked us the question, and we could not have answered. They like to catch us when they can."

"There are other interesting things about the river," said Dorus. "But you, of course, know about them."

"Tell us," responded Brasidas. "We may not know, and even if we do, 'twill do no harm to hear of them again."

"Yes, do tell us," added Chartas, for he had already learned that Dorus was a good storyteller.

"We all know of Helen, wife of King Menelaus of Sparta," said Dorus. "We know that she was stolen by Paris and taken to the city of Troy; and that the siege of Troy, of which Homer tells in the Iliad, was for the purpose of restoring Helen to her husband and to Sparta. That much we learn from Homer."

Chartas and Brasidas nodded, but they did not interrupt.

"But did you know," continued Dorus, "that farther below us, on the Eurotas, there is a temple dedicated to this same Helen?"

"No," exclaimed Chartas and Brasidas together. "How far is it? Can we not go to it to-day?"

"Hardly, to-day, I think," said Dorus, "but perhaps Orestes will take all our company some day, and let us follow the river to the sea. That would be an expedition worth while!"

"It is twenty miles!" exclaimed Brasidas. "Could we return by nightfall?"

"Possibly," said Chartas, "or we might stay over the night and have more time to look over the country, and to see the old temples and statues."

"You have heard of the underground cemetery of Castor and Pollux, and of the temple erected to them?" asked Dorus.

"Yes," replied Chartas, "but I never have seen them. Tell us the story of the Twin Brothers, Dorus, before we return to the city."

"'Tis not fair," said Dorus. "You and Brasidas can tell stories as well as I."

"Brasidas, then!" cried Chartas. "Tell us the story, Brasidas!"

"I would rather run a race, or wrestle, than tell a story," laughed Brasidas, but for all that he began:

"Castor and Pollux," he said, "were twin brothers, sons of Zeus. Castor was a famous horseman, and Pollux was a wrestler. They both sailed with Jason when he went in search of the Golden Fleece. They had power over the winds and the sea.

"Pollux, only, was immortal, and when his Twin Brother died, he begged Zeus, his father, that he be allowed to divide his brother's fate. Zeus gave consent, and for a long time the Twin Brothers alternated between life and death. But later, Zeus set them together among the stars of the heavens. To this day the images of these gods are carried by our kings when they go into war."

"And it was their images that the colonists asked for, a while ago," added Chartas, "when the war was going against them."

"Yes," assented Brasidas. "The request nearly caused a riot in the Assembly!"

"It is the tomb of the Twin Brothers that we will see down the river," said Dorus.

"I am more eager than ever for the trip," said Chartas. "I will ask Orestes to take our company."

"Good! good!" exclaimed the boys. "He will be sure to do it if you ask him."

CHAPTER XIII

DAYS OF PREPARATION

All Sparta was interested in the approaching celebration of the Carnea. This was a war-like festival to the god Apollo, who was regarded as the leader and founder of the Dorians, the race to which the Spartans belonged. He was worshipped as their chief god, and all the principal temples of the country were sacred to him.

Apollo was called the "far darting god," whose arrows never missed their mark. He was said to encourage the warriors, and "with a cloud wrapped about his shoulders," to lead them into the thick of battle.

Apollo was also regarded as the punisher of evil, and the avenger of wrong. He was most beloved of all the gods, for he was believed to be the most friendly to man, protecting him from evil, and healing him in sickness.

Many were the questions which the men of Sparta put to the boys during the days of preparation for the festival, for these celebrations were not intended to be simply a time of fun and frolic. They were regarded as a religious ceremony, pleasing to the god in whose honor they were given. For this reason the boys were expected to know the stories of the gods, and to understand the meaning of all the ceremonies connected with the celebration.

Outside the city, tents were being erected, and the plain on which they stood looked like the encampment of a miniature army.

There were nine tents in all. Each tent was to be occupied by nine men, who would live as though in a military camp, and the celebration would last for nine days.

The boys spent all their spare time watching the preparations for the festival. They saw the tents erected; they knew how they were furnished, and what men were to occupy each one. As they went about the plain, they amused themselves by imagining that they were visiting the tents of a great army, and that they, themselves, were soldiers.

As a group of the boys returned, one day, from an inspection of the camp, they took an unfrequented path that led them back to the city by a longer way.

"I heard a new story, this morning," said Chartas, as they walked on. "One of the soldiers told it to me. I liked it."

"Tell us! tell us!" exclaimed the boys in chorus.

"The story was of Sous, one of the warriors in the early days of Sparta. He was a king, and a real Spartan hero," said Chartas, with shining eyes. "One day he and his warriors were surrounded by their enemies. They had been fighting and marching on a hot day, without a drop of water to drink. Sous and his soldiers were almost perishing from thirst.

"In the valley, guarded by the enemy, there was a fountain of pure water. His soldiers were begging for a drink, and Sous knew that unless his men could obtain water, they must die. So he shouted, ` I will give up all my conquests if I, and my army, are but allowed to drink at your fountain.'

"His enemies were glad to recover so easily what they had lost, and they agreed.

"As the soldiers of Soils were about to rush to the fountain, he cried, ` Hold! I will give my crown to the man who can deny himself water to drink.'

"But the soldiers rushed on, and almost fought for the precious water which they had been so long without.

"Sous stood by and looked at them. Then, dipping his hand in the fountain, he moistened his skin with the water, and turned away without drinking.

"`I still can deny myself,' he said.' The crown is mine! ' "

"Fine! fine!" exclaimed the boys, as Chartas finished.

"That is a good story," said Theognis, "and it was well told."

"Chartas will yet rival you in story-telling, if you are not careful," said Brasidas.

"Oh," replied Theognis, "he is already a worthy rival."

"Have you another story as good as that?" asked Dorus.

"No," replied Chartas with a laugh. "But perhaps some one else has."

No one volunteered, and just then Gelon gave a hasty exclamation.

"Look at that miserable hut!" he said. "Who can live in such a place? But see," he added, "there is a man coming out of the door."

The boys looked, and at once their gaze was held by the strange appearance of the man.

The men of Sparta wore their hair long, while that of the slaves was cropped close. But the hair of this man was long upon one side of his head, and cut close upon the other. His cloak hung upon him in rags.

He was hurrying along the path now, his eyes upon the ground. The boys were strangely quiet. As he drew near to them, he glanced up, and, seeing them, he stepped aside, and, with downcast eyes, waited for them to pass.

For some time longer the boys were silent as they walked on. Then Theron spoke. "Who is he?"

"A deserter!" said Dorus. "Did you not notice his half-cropped head? I remember of hearing my father tell about him. He ran away from the army during an attack. He might better have been killed, for then he would have been a hero. Now he is an outlaw. He cannot live in the city. No one will give him fire for his hearth. He cannot vote; he can take no part in the games or the festivals. No one will wrestle with him in the gymnasium. He lives alone."

"He even made way for us in the path!" exclaimed Theognis.

"Yes," added Dorus, "and if he were witnessing a game and one of us had no seat, he would have to give up his."

"What a terrible life!" exclaimed Brasidas. "So that is what it means to be a deserter from the Spartan army!"

"I have heard," said Chartas, "of a deserter who afterward rushed headlong into the most dangerous place in a battle in order that he might be killed."

"I should think that they would all do that!" exclaimed Gelon.

"So should I," responded Theron.

"Fortunately," said Dorus, "there are not many deserters from the Spartan army."

CHAPTER XIV

THE CARNEA

In the early morning, a group of young girls might have been seen climbing some of the lower slopes of the hills. It was the first day of Apollo. Among the girls were Melissa, Chartas' sister, and Gorgo, who had driven her chariot so fearlessly at the last festival.

"I know where there are late roses in blossom," said Melissa. "Come with me, and I will show you." A group of the girls followed, as she climbed a nearby hill.

"Oh, how beautiful!" they exclaimed, as they came upon the bushes, bending with fragrant blossoms.

They filled their arms with the clusters, and when they could carry no more, they started back toward the city.

Others of the girls joined them as they went on.

"What lovely trailing vines you have found, Gorgo," said Melissa, as they met.

"But not more lovely than your roses," replied Gorgo.

The girls made a beautiful picture with their light draperies and fresh flowers. They seated themselves upon the ground and began fashioning garlands and sprays of bloom, while they talked of the festival, and of the part that they were to take.

"THE GIRLS MADE A BEAUTIFUL PICTURE WITH THEIR LIGHT
DRAPERIES AND FRESH FLOWERS."

"There are strangers in the city," said Gorgo, as she laid aside a garland. "I wish they would not come to our festivals."

"Why do you wish that?" questioned young girl, who sat beside her.

"Because," replied Gorgo, "they think it strange that we take part in the contests and the choruses. In Athens, only the men take part. The girls must stay at home. And when they do go upon the street, they must wear veils over their faces, and speak to no one."

"And do you think these strangers are from Athens?" asked Melissa.

"Yes," answered Gorgo, "I think so. They wear embroidered cloaks, and jeweled ornaments, and they talk and laugh like girls."

"But they are young, are they not?" asked another of the girls.

"They are not boys," replied Gorgo. "But you will doubtless see them for yourselves. Come," she added, rising, "it is time we returned, and our garlands are finished."

The statue of the Carnean Apollo was of wood, and for many, many years it had stood, uncovered by any temple. But it was for this rude wooden image that the girls of Sparta were preparing their offerings of flowers and garlands.

At the sound of flute and cithara, they hastened and took their places in the procession.

As the girls advanced with graceful steps and gestures, and laid their offerings upon the altar of the god, the people sang a joyous chorus of thanksgiving for the peace and plenty that Sparta had enjoyed.

The nine days of the festival were filled with sacrifices, processions, military drills, and music. It was a time of rejoicing for all the people, and especially for the boys of Sparta, for they were trained to be soldiers, and the war-like character of the Carnea pleased them mightily.

Some of the boys lingered beside the altar, after the exercises of the day.

"Think how long this image has stood!" exclaimed Theognis, as he threw himself upon the grass and picked up a flower which had fallen from one of the garlands.

"'Tis said," replied Chartas, stretching himself upon the ground beside Theognis, "that it stood here when Menelaus and Helen ruled. It must have witnessed the stealing away of Helen."

"Yes," added Dorus, "and the setting out of the fleet to bring her back from Troy."

"It makes the poems of Homer seem more real, to think of that," said Brasidas. "Perhaps it will be easier for me to remember my lines if I think of them in connection with the Sparta that I know, and of this image, which was standing then."

One part of the festival was given up to musical contests, both of singers and of those who played upon instruments, and the victors were crowned with wreaths of laurel. It was for honor that they sang, not for gifts, and the laurel wreath won for its wearer the praise and honor of all.

"I wonder if I shall ever be crowned a victor in such contests," said Theognis to himself. "Oh, I hope that I may!"

He had been thrilled by the music of the choruses, but the singing of the men who, one by one, competed for the prize, had stirred him even more.

No one knew Theognis' secret, but he had composed more than one song, which he stole away by himself to sing. No one else had heard them, but often when the boys of his company were sent to forage or to hunt, he went quietly away, and it was then that he sang his songs. His voice was strong, sweet, and flexible, and this the boys of his company knew, for they heard him sing in the choruses. Orestes alone guessed that Theognis would some day be a poet, but it was to Chartas only that he had told his belief—and Chartas had almost forgotten what he had said.

It was near the close of the festival that the foot-race of the girls took place. It was a beautiful sight, and the Spartans loved beauty, though only a free, rugged beauty pleased them.

The girls were dressed in soft white garments, and they ran like the swift, free children of nature that they were. The matrons of Sparta, their faces veiled, watched the contest.

"What would our sisters in Athens say to such sport as this?" exclaimed one of the strangers of whom Gorgo had spoken.

"They would wish to live in Sparta, I think," replied another of the group.

"But not when they had tasted the Spartan black broth and barley bread!" exclaimed a third, with a laugh.

"That is right," said the second speaker, "although one must admit that the Spartans do not live upon bread and broth only, as our Athenians claim."

"Quite true!" said the first. "But, beware," he added, in a lower tone, "some of these Spartans are scowling upon us even now. We had better hold our tongues."

The festival closed with the singing of a great paean, in which all the people joined.

When it was all over, and the city returned to its usual quiet life, with no tents standing upon the plain, and no crowds or sound of music in the streets, life seemed dull enough to the boys. But they took up their drills, and games, and music, and soon settled down to their everyday life again.

CHAPTER XV

THE TRUCE-BEARERS

"Who are these?" asked Brasidas of Chartas, as two strange men entered Sparta near the close of a summer day. "They must have traveled some distance," he added, noticing their dust-covered cloaks.

"They are travelers, surely," replied Chartas, and then, laying his hand upon Brasidas' arm, he said eagerly, "I wonder—can it be that they are the truce-bearers from Elis?"

"Truly, I believe that they are!" exclaimed Brasidas. "Come, let us follow."

The travelers looked about them with interest, as travelers in a strange city will, and the two eager boys followed.

Presently the men reached the market-place of the city, and entered.

"We can go no farther," said Chartas, in a disappointed tone, as he stopped.

"No," said Brasidas, stopping also. "I have no desire to be flogged for so common-place a reason as entering the market-place. I did not know that Melon was so foolish till yesterday."

"Melon!" said Chartas. "Of Procles' company? What of him?"

"Did you not hear?" asked Brasidas laughingly. "He was flogged last night for entering the market-place. A slave was running from his master, and Melon's curiosity got the better of him, and he followed."

"He must have been curious!" exclaimed Chartas, with an answering laugh. "Was he so anxious to see the slave flogged that he forgot his own safety?"

"I think that, to-day, he will have more sympathy for the slave," chuckled Brasidas. "I wonder," said Chartas, "why it is that we boys are never allowed in the market-place."

"Spartans are not trained for farmers or tradesmen," said Brasidas, "and I suppose if we were allowed there, we would be idle and curious. But, listen," he added, "I believe they are coming back."

Brasidas was right. The two men were now accompanied by some of the magistrates of the city. Before the strangers went a herald who called: "Attend, ye people! The Elean truce-bearers of Zeus address you!"

The people stopped in their various occupations. They came from their homes, and from the temples, and gathered in the streets as the truce-bearers went about proclaiming their message:

"No army may invade another's territory. All must live in peace, that the sacred games at Olympia may be celebrated without interruption or discord."

There was general rejoicing throughout the city, as the

truce-bearers proclaimed their mission, and the approaching games became the chief topic of conversation.

"Your father has been to the games," said Gelon to Chartas, as the boys were together later. "Tell us what it is like at Olympia. He has told you, has he not?"

"Yes," replied Chartas, "but it is better to hear from one who has seen for himself."

"But none of us have been. Tell us what you can," urged the boys.

"Of course we know that everybody goes who can," said Chartas, "and Father says that the roads leading to Olympia are filled with travelers of every age, and every station in life. Some ride, but many more walk.

"At Olympia," he continued, "there is a great temple with an image of Zeus, which is made from ivory and gold. The image is forty feet high. All the people go there with offerings, but those who are to take part in the games go before the image and take oath that they have a right to compete, and that they will use only fair means to win.

"In the groves there are many statues of victors, besides temples and altars to the gods.

"A course is laid out for the games, and the people sit in the seats and upon the hillsides which rise all around it."

"It must be a wonderful festival!" exclaimed Brasidas.

"Yes," continued Chartas, "Father says that it is like a great market-place, too, for merchants bring all kinds of goods there to sell. But our Spartan money is not of much use in buying from foreign merchants, nor have they much to sell that could be used in Sparta. We care too little for luxuries, nor would they be allowed within the city.

"On the last day," Chartas resumed, "there are processions in honor of the victors, and sacrifices of thanksgiving are made to Zeus. Then the city of Elis gives a great banquet in honor of those who have won victories in the games."

"I wish we all might go!" exclaimed Dorus.

"Perhaps some of us may compete at the next Olympiad," said Theognis, and then he blushed under his swarthy skin, because he had spoken his thought.

"Four years is a long time to wait," said Dorus, "but it will give us time to practise the games, and perhaps find out what we can do best."

"I have heard it rumored," said Brasidas, "that Gorgo plans to send her chariot and horses then."

"'Tis too bad that she cannot drive them herself!" cried Gelon. "She handles them like a man."

"Ah, but the best drivers in all Greece are there," said Theron. "'Tis not like our smaller festivals." "That is true," replied Gelon, "but I would wager upon a Spartan maiden against a man of Athens!"

"Good!" cried the boys heartily, although they shouted at the same time with laughter.

"But Gorgo's horses are wonderful!" said Dorus, when they had grown quiet again.

And all the boys agreed, "That is true!"

CHAPTER XVI

"EARTH AND WATER"

"You seem so quiet, Orestes, and so thoughtful. Is anything troubling you?" It was Chartas who spoke, and he looked anxiously into Orestes' face.

Three years have passed since we last saw Chartas, and he is no longer a member of a company of boys, but the captain of a company of his own. The friendship between Orestes and himself has grown with the years, and now there seems less difference between their ages than when they were younger.

"I *am* troubled," Orestes answered. "Not for myself," he added, as Chartas gave a quick gesture of sympathy, "but for Sparta—nay, not for Sparta alone, but for Greece."

"Then you believe the rumors," said Chartas.

"You think the Persians are really likely to invade Greece?"

"Yes," replied Orestes, "I do believe the rumors."

"But even though the Persian numbers are great, as 'tis said," Chartas answered, "they are a barbarian horde. They could not stand against the trained soldiers of Greece."

Orestes smiled at the earnest face of Chartas, but his smile was one of appreciation, not of amusement.

"I hope you are right," he said. "But sometimes I fear it is our own ignorance that makes us feel so secure. Mind," he added, "I do not think we are going to be defeated if the Persians come, but that the struggle will be a much greater one than we Spartans, at least, now realize."

"How have you learned this?" asked Chartas, for Orestes' earnest speech had made a deep impression upon him.

"I have thought much about it," replied Orestes, "and I have asked many questions of those who have traveled abroad."

Chartas was silent. Persia was, to him, an unknown land, as it was to most of the Spartans, who seldom left their own country. His gaze rested upon the road which led from Sparta toward the hills on the farther side of the river, but his thoughts were far beyond the hills.

Suddenly his gaze grew intent, and after a moment he leaned forward, as though to see more clearly. "Who are the men coming yonder?" he asked.

Orestes turned and gazed as earnestly as Chartas had done.

"They are not Spartans," he said. "One can see their rich apparel, and they wear the hats of travelers."

They continued to gaze, and, at length, as the men came close, they exclaimed together, "They are barbarians! They are no Greeks. What does it mean?"

As the men passed on, Chartas and Orestes followed at a distance. The men went straight to the market-place, passed the Temple of Fear, and stopped before the Ephoreum. After looking about them for a moment, they entered the building.

By this time quite a crowd had gathered, for the sight of the two strangers had awakened the curiosity of all.

"Who are they?" "Where are they from?" "What is their business?" These questions were heard upon every side, but no one could answer.

For a long time the people waited, while the crowd increased as the news spread, until it seemed as though every citizen of Sparta was in the throng.

At length the ephors appeared. The strangers were with them. Then these stepped aside, and the two kings of Sparta stepped from the door of the Ephoreum.

"They must have interrupted a session of the ephors," said Chartas, and then he stopped and listened, for one of the kings was speaking.

"Men of Sparta," he said, "King Darius of Persia has sent his ambassadors to demand of us a gift of earth and water."

There was a moment of absolute silence. Then, from every side, there arose an uproar of sound. Men shouted, groaned, shook their fists; there were imprecations, bellowings of wrath, jeers, and oaths. The women who fringed the crowd shrieked, or wailed, or laughed aloud in derision.

The king waited. The ambassadors of Darius first flushed; then grew pale.

"Earth and water!" exclaimed Orestes between set teeth. "It has come! But I wish Darius himself were here. I wonder if he would think the Spartans likely to become his subjects—to pay him tribute!" For this was the meaning of the ambassadors' mission. Earth and water were the signs of surrender.

In the meantime the uproar continued—increased. The sound had brought others from the outskirts of the city. From all directions they were coming,—running, shouting, inquiring. And as they learned the news, they, too, shouted defiance, threw their arms, threatened.

At first the ambassadors had listened to the mob with curling lips and heads thrown back. But as the tumult increased their manner changed. One of them raised his hand, and attempted to speak.

But it was useless. The effort only roused the mob to ridicule; and then threats of violence began to be heard.

"No, no!" cried Orestes, to a man beside him, who was shouting threats against the ambassadors, "remember the honor of Sparta.

Let the ambassadors carry our message to their king."

But it was like trying to stop the flow of a mountain torrent with a man's hand. Not even the kings could stop the mighty outburst of the mob's anger and passion.

There was a sudden surge of the crowd. It swept up the steps of the Ephoreum, and the ambassadors were dragged away.

Later in the day, when the city had grown quiet and the people had gone to their houses,—though they still gathered in small groups here and there, in excited conversation,—Orestes and Chartas walked once more together along the river bank.

A man passed them. With a savage laugh he exclaimed: "Darius will wait long for his ambassadors!"

But Orestes responded: "And Sparta's honor! What of that?"

CHAPTER XVII

A RUNNER FROM MARATHON

"Of what are you thinking, these days?" asked Orestes, as he came upon Chartas walking slowly along a footpath outside the city.

"Of Sparta's lack of readiness for war," answered Chartas frankly. "Even the boys of my company drill but half-heartedly. I think their interests are all upon games and festivals. I am not so good a captain as you were, Orestes."

"I do not hear that from others," replied Orestes with a smile. "But all Sparta is restless," he added, "and I think it is not wholly due to the games."

The sound of rapid footfalls and of panting breath close behind them, made them turn quickly. A man dashed past. His look was strained; he half staggered as he ran; he was covered with dust.

"What news?" cried Orestes, as he passed.

The man turned his head for but one word. "War," he said, hoarsely, as he staggered and ran on.

Orestes and Chartas bounded forward, more fleet of foot, now, than the runner, and when he reached the market-place the people had already been summoned.

"THE MAN TURNED HIS HEAD FOR BUT ONE WORD."

"I have come from Athens," the man gasped. "The Persian army is ready to make an attack. Send troops; send troops, or Greece is lost!" As the man finished he dropped, exhausted, upon the ground.

"Where will the battle be fought?" asked the ephors.

"Marathon," gasped the man. And it was no wonder that he gasped, for it was learned that he had run a distance of one hundred and forty miles in forty-eight hours.

The word spread like fire through the city. "A runner has come from Marathon. The Persian army is ready to attack Athens. They want us to send troops."

There was consternation. It was the time of sacrificing to the gods, and it lacked five days till the full moon. No Spartan army could begin its march till the time of the full moon. What could be done?

"Can the sacrifices be neglected?" asked some.

"What care the Persians for our sacrifices!" exclaimed others. "Will they wait for that? What about Athens?"

"We must help Athens! How can we refuse?" cried Orestes.

"But the sacrifices! We must honor the gods if we hope to win in battle!" said the older men.

"It is yet five days till the moon is full," cried another. "We cannot send our soldiers until then!"

"'Twill take that time to gather our army," another declared—though it was but an excuse to temporize.

The counsel of the older men prevailed, as it always did in

Sparta, and after the long five days of delay the troops were in readiness.

"I am not too young to go," cried Chartas imploringly. "And Sparta has too few men to meet the Persian horde!"

"He is best of all the Pyrrhic war dancers," said one of the men.

"If Orestes goes, we cannot hold him," said another.

And so, when the troops marched away from Sparta, Chartas went by Orestes' side.

After anxious days of waiting, the sounds of fife and cithara were heard advancing from the hills.

The people of Sparta flocked out, and ran far beyond the city to meet the returning army. Would there be few, or many? How had the battle gone?

The entire army was returning! The people shouted for joy.

But the soldiers marched with grim faces.

"We were too late!" exclaimed the general in command, and it was as though he had flung the words in the faces of the people. "We delayed! The battle was fought without us! But," he added, "the Persians were defeated. The gods themselves fought for Greece."

As the army disbanded, groups formed here and there to learn the story in greater detail. Then the people were told how the Athenians, though few in number, had met the Persian host on the plain of Marathon, and had driven them back to their ships. They were told, too, of the size and magnificence of the invading army, and of the rich spoils which were left upon the field.

"Our general said that the gods had a part in the battle," said Theognis. "What did he mean by that?"

"They told us strange stories when we reached the field," said Chartas. "Some of the people declared that the Greek soldiers were encouraged by the god Pan, who shouted and cheered them on from the mountains. Others said that Theseus himself was in the thick of the battle, clad in armor, and fighting mightily against the Persians; and that great Herakles appeared, and drove the barbarians into the water, as men would drive a flock of sheep."

"'Twas a deed bravely done!" exclaimed Orestes. "Would that we might have had a part in it!"

Theognis' face lighted as he listened. Then, when none was noticing, he stole away to the foot-hills. The impulse was strong upon him. He had been stirred by the picture which Chartas' words had called up—of the gods fighting for Greece—and easily, naturally, he began to put the pictures into words, and then to sing. As the pictures grew more distinct, so the words of his song fashioned themselves more readily, until his voice rose clearly, freely, in a song of triumph, a paean of thanksgiving.

"Hark!" said Orestes softly, for he and Chartas had strolled away from the noisy groups. "'Tis the voice of Theognis."

"Truly it is," said Chartas. "But what is his song? I have not heard it."

"No?" questioned Orestes, with an odd smile. "What have I told you, Chartas?"

For a moment Chartas looked puzzled, and then his face lighted. With a gasp of astonishment he asked: "Do you think the song is his own?"

"Listen," said Orestes again, and now they heard the words, as Theognis sang of the battle—of the aid of the gods in the battle.

"'Tis his own!" cried Chartas in delight. "Oh, Orestes, he must sing at the festival!"

"I hope that he will," said Orestes, "but we must bide his own time."

That night, as the men sat in barracks after their evening meal, Theognis took his cithara and began to sing. It was his own song of the battle.

The men listened; they leaned forward; unconsciously they began to beat the time, and when the song was finished, voices arose shouting, "Victor! victor!"

There was no laurel wreath with which to crown him, but Theognis was satisfied, for he knew that his song was approved; that his gift was recognized.

The song was called for again, and yet again. Then others began to sing it with him, until finally all the voices joined in the new paean of thanksgiving.

"Ah, Theognis," said Chartas, as soon as he could join him, "Orestes has been waiting for this, but I was stupid. I did not know."

"Orestes!" exclaimed Theognis in surprise. "How should he know?"

"Oh," replied Chartas, "he has understood you. But I was blind!"

"But, Chartas," said Theognis, grasping his hand, "it was you who aroused me at last. It was you who gave me the subject for my song!"

CHAPTER XVIII

FOR SPARTA'S HONOR

Once more the truce-bearers of Olympia had come to Sparta with their message of peace.

"Let us pray the gods that we may be able to keep the truce!" exclaimed Orestes.

"But the games are in honor of the gods," said Theognis. "We cannot hope for victory in war, if we fail to honor the gods."

"'Tis true enough!" replied Orestes thoughtfully.

"You are going to the games?" questioned Chartas of Theognis. "You must go," he added, "and enter the musical contest with your song."

"Yes," answered Theognis, "I am going, and—" he flushed as he added, "I hope to sing."

"Many who were of our old company are going," said Gelon. "You are of course," he added. "You have trained for the foot-race."

"Yes, I have trained," replied Chartas, but he said no more.

"Gorgo is sending her chariot and horses!" exclaimed Dorus. "I hope they will win."

It was later in the day when Chartas again met some of his

friends, and again the subject of the Olympic games was mentioned. The boys had not understood his apparent indifference of the morning, for he had taken his many months of training for the foot-race with such enthusiasm and perseverance that they all had predicted that he would win. And now, when he said, in answer to a question from Gelon, "I shall not compete," they were too greatly surprised even to speak.

Chartas looked into their faces. He had hoped to be able to show them what Orestes had shown him, of the danger that threatened Greece: of the need of standing ready for instant action. The battle of Marathon, too, had opened his eyes to the size and character of the Persian army, and he knew that the defeat of the Persians there would by no means end the invasion; and of this, too, he had hoped to convince them.

But what Chartas saw when he looked into the faces of his friends held him speechless. It was a dawning look of distrust; even of scorn.

Could it be that these friends, with whom he had lived day by day, through all the years of his boyhood and youth, could believe for a moment that he was a coward? So the faces told him!

With a suffocating, choking sense of resentment, anger, hurt, he turned and strode away. He could not speak, nor would he, now.

"I have no heart for the games this year," said Orestes, later, when he and Chartas were alone together. "If it were not that you are to compete, I should not go."

"But I shall not compete," said Chartas quietly. "I have already withdrawn." He turned his face, that Orestes might not see its expression, for his hurt was still fresh and keen.

"What! Not compete? And you have trained for the foot-race, and are almost sure to win!" cried Orestes.

"I had thought to go," said Chartas, "but even though it is the time of the truce, something tells me that Sparta will have need of men at home."

It was some moments before Orestes answered. Then he laid his arm across Chartas' shoulders with the old gesture, as he said, "It must have been a hard struggle to give it up. Aye, it took courage, more than most of your age could summon! But, Chartas, you are right. What do the Persian hordes care for the sacred games of Greece?

"But, listen!" he added. "The heralds are summoning the people. Let us see what it means."

Together they hurried to the place of assembly.

As soon as the people had gathered, one of the aged senators stood forth. There was a hush over all as he began to speak.

"Men of Sparta," he said, "we are soon to send competitors to the Olympic games, in honor of the gods. Can the gods accept the offerings of those who are dishonored?"

"No!" shouted the people. "No!"

"But we are dishonored!" exclaimed the senator, his voice ringing as he flung out the words. "In the heat of passion we have slain two innocent men."

There was a murmur at this, partly of approval, partly of disapproval. But he went on.

"The men came as ambassadors. They bore a message from their king. Had we acted with honor, we would have sent them back—empty-handed, to be sure—but we would have sent them back to their king.

"But Sparta has a conscience," he continued, "and Sparta's conscience is at length aroused. We must wipe out the stain upon our honor!"

"Yes, yes!" cried many voices among the throng, while others shouted, "How can we do it?"

"There is but one way," said the aged man. He was silent as his gaze swept over the up-turned faces of the multitude. "But one way!" he repeated slowly. Then, after an impressive pause, he added: "We must send two men to Darius, to fare at his hands as his ambassadors did at ours!"

There was a breathless silence.

Then there was a movement among the crowd, and at almost the same instant four Spartans stood before the senator, and as one man they said: "I will go. For Sparta's honor, I will go."

The senator looked at the men. "Sperthias, Bulis, Orestes, Chartas!" he cried. "But two are needed. The lot shall be cast."

Again Orestes' arm rested upon Chartas' shoulder, as he whispered, "Pray the gods that we may go together!"

But it was not to be. The lot was cast, and the names of Sperthias and Bulls were called.

There was no shout. A feeling of solemnity fell upon the people, as they realized the price that must be paid for their rash and dishonorable act.

Quietly they dispersed, talking in low undertones, and with grave faces.

Chartas felt a hand placed upon his arm. Turning, he faced his father, and beside Danaus were his mother and Melissa.

Melissa caught his hand, and held it close, while his mother threw her arms about him—but said no word.

"My son," said Danaus simply, "you have made us both proud and happy."

Then a group of young men sought out Orestes and Chartas. Turning toward the group, the friends stood in the attitude so familiar to them all.

Dorus was the first to speak.

"Chartas," he said, "yesterday, after you left us, I called you a coward, because you withdrew from the foot-race. I thought you feared the trial. Now I hate myself for having had such a thought. I should have known you better!"

"We should all have known you better," cried Theron and Gelon.

"And I!" exclaimed Brasidas, pressing forward. "After all the years we have been together, even I wondered if you lacked courage." His face flushed. "Courage!" he added, with intense self-scorn, *"and you would have died for Sparta's honor!"*

THE END.

Made in United States
Orlando, FL
26 September 2023